Calvin Coconut
MAN TRIP

Kauai

Start Here
Oahu

Molokai

Lanai

Maui

↓ Land Here

HAWAii

Other Books About
Calvin Coconut

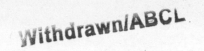

CALVIN COCONUT

MAN TRIP

Graham Salisbury

illustrated by

Jacqueline Rogers

A yearling Book

All rights reserved. Published in the United States by Yearling, an imprint of Random House Children's Books, a division of Random House, Inc., New York. Originally published in hardcover in the United States by Wendy Lamb Books, an imprint of Random House Children's Books, New York, in 2012.

Yearling and the jumping horse design are registered trademarks of Random House, Inc.

Visit us on the Web! randomhouse.com/kids

Educators and librarians, for a variety of teaching tools, visit us at RHTeachersLibrarians.com

The Library of Congress has cataloged the hardcover edition of this work as follows:
Salisbury, Graham.
Calvin Coconut : man trip / by Graham Salisbury ; illustrated by Jacqueline Rogers. – 1st ed.
p. cm.
Summary: Fourth-grader Calvin flies from Oahu to the big island of Hawaii to go on a deep-sea fishing trip with Ledward, his mother's boyfriend, and learns to appreciate other living creatures–especially one enormous marlin.
ISBN 978-0-385-73964-1 (trade) – ISBN 978-0-385-90798-9 (lib. bdg.)
ISBN 978-0-375-89797-9 (ebook) [1. Big game fishing–Fiction. 2. Fishing–Fiction. 3. Human-animal relationships–Fiction. 4. Family life–Hawaii–Fiction. 5. Hawaii–Fiction.]
I. Rogers, Jacqueline, ill. II. Title. III. Title: Man trip.
PZ7.S15225Cadm 2012
[Fic]–dc23
2011010959

ISBN 978-0-375-86507-7 (pbk.)

Printed in the United States of America

For my Big Island pal
and Hawaii Prep classmate,
"Baja" Bill Jardine
—G.S.

For my brothers,
Bob and Marty
—J.R.

1

TOSSING BUFOS

Every time my mom calls me her little man of the house, I slip out the back door and run down to my friend Julio's. "Man of the house" means: "Time to clean your room," or "Take out the garbage," or worst of all, "Cut the grass."

This time it was the grass.

I glanced at the door.

Mom hooked her finger into the collar of my T-shirt. "Oh no you don't. You've let that grass grow far too long. You need to cut it. Now."

Dang.

"Aw, come on, Mom, I hate that job."

"We all have to do things we don't like. Now, I filled the gas can at the service station. You have everything you need to get that old lawn mower started. Bye."

I hung my head and made a big show of how hard this was for me. I mean, jeese, I could have been at the beach. "You're killing me, Mom."

She pointed her finger. "Go."

I went out to the garage.

Actually, cutting the grass wasn't hard. It was just disgusting.

Who wanted to go out there and shred

2

bufos? Bufos are toads, big fat juicy ones. And when the grass got long they came up from the river and dug down into it to sleep. Unless you got down on your hands and knees to look for them, you couldn't see where they were. But the lawn mower could, and it spat shredded bufo guts all over my feet, every time.

I poured gas into the tank and rolled our cranky mower out into the sun.

It was hot as a frying pan. Nothing moved, except my dog, Streak, who was lounging in the shade under Mom's car. She lifted her head but didn't get up.

"Hey," I said to her. "You want to help?"

Streak yawned and went back to sleep.

"Lazybones."

I looked out over our front yard and all that grass sloping down to the river that ran by our house. Mom was right; I'd let it grow too long. It was so long I wondered if it was even *possible* to cut it. Man, I thought, there have to be a hundred toads in there.

I pushed the mower to the edge of the driveway.

"Now'd be a good time to wake up and run for it, bufos," I said. "That is, if you know what's good for you."

I could almost hear them snoring.

Up the street, Julio's house slept in the Saturday-morning stillness. Julio wasn't out cutting *his* grass. Nobody else was out there, either. The place was a ghost town.

I looked back at my dog. "Maybe everyone heard Mom say 'man of the house' and ran for it, Streak."

Who could blame them if they had? Sometimes I got Julio or Willy to take a turn at cutting the grass. They didn't mind . . . until they got splattered with toad guts. Tito and Bozo came wandering down our street once when I was mowing. They didn't care about the grass, but they loved the toad guts. "Ho, so gross!" Tito said. "I like it."

Tito and Bozo were sixth graders at my school. I tried to stay away from them because they liked to cause trouble.

Yeah, well, this lawn mower was trouble. I yanked the pull cord.

The engine spat, shuddered, and died.

I tried again. This time it coughed out a cloud of stinky smoke.

But it stayed on.

I covered my ears. The thing was as loud as six guys on motorcycles, gunning their engines and flexing their tattoos.

Streak got up and loped around to the back

of the house. "Oh, great," I called. "Just leave me here by myself."

I started mowing by the driveway and inched my way down the slope toward the river. I had to push a foot, then pull back, then push, then pull. Inch by inch. Otherwise the grass would clog the blades and kill the engine.

Things were going fine for about five minutes.

Then, *spluuurt!*

"Ahh!"

I leaped back, letting go of the mower.

"Dang it!" My bare feet were painted with the remains of some sleeping bufo who never knew what hit him. "I hate this!"

I left the mower growling and ran up to the house to squirt my feet off with the hose.

"I saw that," Mom said, poking her head out the screen door. "You've got to chase all the toads out of the grass first."

"It's hopeless, Mom. There are too many,

and anyway, it would take me all day. And you can't see them. The grass is too deep."

"Calvin. You can't just chop them up! That's cruel." She shook her head and went back inside.

"Yeah, I know," I mumbled. "I'll chase them out."

The ones I could find, anyway.

I killed the engine and left the lawn mower sitting halfway down the slope.

"Dang toads," I muttered.

But Mom was right. I couldn't just kill them. And anyway I didn't want to.

I started searching the grass.

The way I found them was with my feet. They were squishy when you stepped on them. Creepy, but it worked.

"Yuck!" I said, step-
ping on my first snor-
ing victim.

I reached down
and dug him out. He
was fat, soft, and ugly.

I held him up and looked him in the eye. "This is your lucky day, toady. You live to catch another fly."

That day when Tito and Bozo watched me, Tito said that if I didn't like all the guts I should dig out the toads and throw them into the river. "They like the water," he said. "Throw um high. Like a baseball. They like that, too."

"No they don't." I didn't believe him.

"Sure they do. Try it and see. They just kick back to shore."

He was right. They just swam back into the swamp grass.

"Okay, toad," I said now. "Here you go!"

I tossed the toad in a high arc into the water. It landed with a splat and floated for a few seconds, unmoving. Then it woke up and kicked to shore. How can they like that? I wondered.

I shrugged and started looking for another one.

By the time Ledward drove up in his old army jeep, I'd tossed eight toads into the river. Ledward was my mom's boyfriend. He was a giant Hawaiian guy who had a banana farm up in the mountains.

Ledward shut the jeep down and got out. He grinned. "You looking for bufos in the grass?"

I nodded. "I gotta get them out so I can cut it."

I felt around with my foot and found another one. I pulled it out and catapulted it into the river.

Splat!

It took a while to recover.

"Maybe you should carry them down to the water?" Ledward said.

I looked back at him. "Why?"

"Well, that one hit kind of hard. What

you're doing could hurt them. Maybe even kill them. Did you think about that?"

"No."

"Well . . ."

Ledward studied me a moment, then went into the house.

2

your Friend, Shayla

Just before lunch on Monday, I was sitting at my desk in Mr. Purdy's room as school dragged on. At home, I hadn't mowed any more grass, but I'd dug up fourteen toads and sent them swimming.

I shook my head, thinking of all the grass

I still had to cut. And now it had grown two days longer. Prob'ly all the bufos I'd dug up had already come back, too.

I frowned. What if what Ledward said about me hurting them was true? Would those ones come back?

I looked up at the clock. Ten minutes till lunch.

Mr. Purdy was standing over by Willy on the other side of the room, talking about something.

Outside, the sky was blue. I could feel the sun's heat coming into the classroom. My desk was in the front row, on the end by the window. I had the best seat you could get.

Almost.

To my left I could gaze out and see the schoolyard. In front of me was Manly Stanley, a centipede who was our class pet and lived in a terrarium on Mr. Purdy's desk. And behind me, I could look back and see my goofy friend, Rubin.

Everything was perfect.

Except for what was on my right.

"Hi, Calvin," Shayla said.

She reached over to drop a folded-up piece of paper on my desk.

I stared at it, then slowly picked it up and opened it.

A cartoon frog decorated the top. A *frog*! I couldn't get away from them!

Shayla's had a bow on its head.

Jeese.

Below the frog, she'd written:

Dear Calvin,

My mom finally said I could get a dog. Can you tell me where you got the one you brought to class that one time? I want to get one just like yours.

Your friend, Shayla . . . in the next seat

My *friend*?

I crumpled the note in my fist and glanced

around the room, looking for help, a distraction or something. Anything.

I turned and looked back at Rubin, but he was busy picking his nose. Julio dozed at his desk by the door.

Shayla turned around, too. "What are you looking at?"

"Nothing."

She reached over and poked my arm. "I really like your dog. What kind is it? Do you think there's another one like it? Was it in a box of puppies? Did you get it at a store? Did it cost money? Was—"

I closed my eyes and took a breath. "I got my dog at the Humane Society. Ledward took me."

"What's the Humane Society?"

"It's where they keep lost cats and dogs."

"Oh. Well, do you have the address?"

"Uh—"

We jumped when we realized Mr. Purdy was standing there listening. "You two think you could wait until lunch to finish your conversation?"

Heat washed over my face. Mr. Purdy wasn't the only one looking at us. The entire class was!

Julio was grinning like a fool.

Willy flicked his eyebrows.

Maya rolled her eyes.

Rubin made a kissy face and gave me a thumbs-up.

~~~   *~~~*   *~~~*

"Hey," Julio said out in the schoolyard after lunch.

We were sitting in the shade of a monkey-pod tree—me, Julio, Rubin, and Willy. The sun was burning everything in sight.

Shayla was with two girls across the way by the drinking fountain. All three of them were peeking over at us and whispering.

"So listen," Julio said, "why don't you invite your girlfriend over to sit with us? We don't mind if you like Shayla."

"Shuddup!"

He laughed.

"Look," he said, lifting his chin toward them. "They're talking about you."

"No, they're talking about *you* because of how you're so ugly."

Everyone cracked up.

When Shayla started walking over to us, I scrambled to my feet and ran for my life.

3

Tickets

That night after dinner, headlights flashed through our front window. My little sister, Darci, and I were sitting on the living room floor.

Darci was watching cartoons, and I was sitting next to her, trying to figure out how to tie a bowline knot with a piece of rope.

Ledward parked his jeep, jumped out, and hurried to the screen door.

Something was up.

He burst into the house waving an envelope. "Your mom around? Got something to show her."

"Out back with Stella," I said. Stella was a girl who came from Texas to live with us, help Mom, and go to high school.

Ledward dipped his head at the rope in my hands. "Whatchoo doing?"

"Trying to tie a bowline. What's in the envelope?"

"Tickets."

"For what?"

"Not for what . . . for *where*."

Ledward turned as Mom and Stella came back in.

"Well, this is a surprise," Mom said.

She gave Ledward a peck on his cheek, then looked at me. "You just going to leave that lawn mower sitting out there in the yard, or are you going to finish what you started?"

"Uh . . . there's too many–"

"The toads are no excuse."

"Yeah," I mumbled. "I'll finish, Mom."

"He's been tossing them into the river," Ledward said. "I told him I wasn't so sure that was a good idea."

Mom cocked her head. "Tossing what into the river?"

"Bufos."

Stella gave me a look that said: Now, this is interesting.

Mom turned to me. "Really? Tossing them, or just letting them loose in the water?"

Now Stella's grin said: Let's see you get out of this one.

I squirmed. Why did Ledward have to bring that up? "They're just toads, Mom. And anyway, Tito said they like it."

Stella snickered.

"Tito?" Mom said. "That boy who's always in trouble?"

Mom looked at Ledward.

Ledward cleared his throat. "I have an idea. But first, I have something for you."

"Oh?"

He pulled the tickets out and held them up. "Remember you wanted to take Darci to Kauai to visit your mother? Well, here you go, courtesy of Hawaiian Airlines."

He handed her the tickets.

"Wow! Where'd you get these?"

Stella peeked over Mom's shoulder.

"Won them," Ledward said. "There was a promotion at my bank. I put my name in a box and bingo! I won. With these tickets you can fly anytime, anywhere in the islands."

"Well, aren't you the lucky one. And you're giving them to *us*?"

Mom threw her arms around him, waving the tickets. "Darci, look. Ledward hit the jackpot!"

Darci turned away from the TV. "What?"

"Ledward won some airline tickets and he's giving them to us. Isn't he sweet? Now we can go see Nana."

Darci jumped up, grinning.

Mom shuffled the tickets. "There are four of them. We'd only need two, unless you want to come, too, Calvin."

"No, no. I'm fine." I didn't want to get trapped doing girl stuff with Mom and Darci.

"Hey, wait," Stella said. "Can you fly to California with those tickets? I want to go to Hollywood. And then New York, and stop in Texas on the way."

Ledward hesitated. "I don't think Hawaiian Airlines flies to–"

"She's joking," Mom said.

"Oh. Yeah. Sure."

Mom leaned her head against Ledward's chest. He was way taller than her. "Thank you, Led. It's so thoughtful of you to share these with us."

Ledward put his arm around her as the phone rang.

"I'll get it." Stella ran to the kitchen.

"Hello," she sang, probably thinking it was her boyfriend, Clarence.

She covered the receiver with her hand and stretched the phone cord toward me from the kitchen doorway. "For you."

"Who is it?"

"Some girl."

I froze. "Girl?"

"The name Shayla mean anything to you?"

4

Junk Fish

Think.

"Uh ... uh ... tell her I'm not here," I whispered.

"Calvin!" Mom whispered back. "Answer that phone."

Stella raised a clenched fist. "I will *not* tell her you're not here, and unless you want some

Texas Nice, microchild, you'd better come here and talk to this girl."

Texas Nice was something Stella always threatened me and Darci with. I figured it was a hard slug in the arm. But she'd never followed through with it.

Not yet, anyway.

Still . . . Shayla?

I ran toward the front door. "I gotta go find Streak . . . and . . . and . . . and feed her. She must be starving."

Even though I'd already fed her.

"Oh, right," Stella said, low. "Just run away. *Coward.*"

"No, I just gotta feed my dog!"

"Calvin, you come back here and answer the phone," Mom said.

"Streak!" I called, banging the screen door open.

I ran out into the night.

Looking back through the window, I could see Stella talking to Shayla. What was she saying?

After school a couple of days later, Julio and I were down by the river with bamboo fishing poles catching aholehole, which are spikey-finned little silver fish. We'd caught six, and they were roasting in the sun next to us on the thick deep grass.

The lawn mower sat up the slope behind us, exactly where I'd left it. I felt guilty for not finishing. But I'd do it later.

I'd mostly managed to avoid Shayla, too, but not the frogs with bows that she kept leaving on my desk.

The bufos in my yard were the opposite of cute. Maybe I'd bring one to school and give it to her. She'd scream her head off.

"What are you grinning at?" Julio said.

"Uh . . . nothing."

Julio hooked another aholehole. "Hoo! Cool, yeah, when they tug on the line?"

"I know. That's the best part."

Now we had seven fish roasting in the sun. I heard the sound of Ledward's jeep.

He waved and got out with a bundle of yellow flowers wrapped in green leaves.

"Fish biting?" he said, heading down to me and Julio.

I nodded. "Just these small ones."

He crouched over the seven aholeholes on the grass. "I see."

Julio stuck more bait on his hook. "They're biting bacon today."

Ledward chuckled. "That always worked for me, too."

I lifted my chin toward the flowers. "Smells good. What are they for?"

"Yellow ginger. For your mom." He glanced at the empty garage. "Not home yet, huh?"

"Soon, prob'ly."

Ledward watched us fish for a few minutes. "What you going do with these aholeholes?"

I shrugged.

"Feed um to the ants," Julio said. "They're junk fish."

Ledward frowned. "If they're junk fish, why don't you just throw them back in the water after you catch them?"

We both looked at Ledward. Throw the fish *back*?

"You just killing them for no reason."

I looked at Julio. Who threw fish back? Nobody I knew.

Julio raised his eyebrows.

"Was me," Ledward said, standing up, "I'd throw them back. If you not going eat um, let um live, ah?" He smiled. "Hey. Gotta get these flowers in some water."

He headed back up to the house.

Julio looked at me.

"I know," I said. "Weird."

27

5

MAN Trip

A few minutes later Mom drove up and pulled into the garage. She got out and went right into the house. Good. If she saw that lawn mower sitting in the same place, she'd say, "The man of the house always finishes what he starts."

I frowned. I wasn't much of a man of the house.

Julio pulled up his line and wound it around his bamboo pole.

"Take the fish," I said.

"What for?"

"I don't know. Give them to Maya's cat?"

"Pshh. Just throw um in the bushes for the mongooses."

"What you're saying is you're lazy?"

"Bingo!"

Julio flicked his eyebrows and left.

I tossed the seven dried-out fish into the bushes and smelled the fish stink on my fingers. Some lucky mongoose would have a feast.

When I put my fishing pole back in the garage, Streak was sitting there with a tennis ball in her mouth.

I laughed. "You're kidding, right?" Streak was the laziest ball fetcher on the planet.

She dropped the ball.

"All right," I said. "But you better bring it back to me, and I mean all the way, got it?"

Streak ran out into the yard.

I picked up the ball and tossed it toward the river. Streak bounded down after it and brought it back . . . halfway.

She dropped it and sat.

I walked down to pick it up.

I squatted to scratch her chin. "Lazy dog, you are something else, you know?"

Just then, Ledward came out and waved to me. "I have an idea."

I stood, tossing the ball up and down. "What kind of idea?"

"Come," he said, nodding toward the river. "Let's sit."

We sat side by side on the grass. I tossed the ball from one hand to the other.

For a minute no one said anything.

"Who's Shayla?" Ledward asked.

"What?"

"The girl who called you?"

"Uh . . . she's just a . . . girl. She won't leave me alone. It's kind of a problem."

"That's not a problem."

"You don't know Shayla."

Ledward chuckled.

He glanced at the lawn mower. "What about that?"

I looked up in fake surprise. "Oh. Yeah. Forgot."

Ledward laughed but said, "Be good if you finish that job. Your mom counts on your help." He crossed his arms over his knees. "What'd you do with the fish?"

I lifted my chin toward the bushes. Ants were probably crawling all over them by now. "In there."

Ledward said nothing. Then, "I've been thinking. You know those tickets I won?"

"Yeah. Hawaiian Airlines."

"Got two left, and I think you and me should take a trip, too. A man trip."

I sat up. "Man trip?"

Ledward smiled. "Me, I try to get away once in a while, just to rest my head. Sometimes I go by myself. Sometimes I go with some guys I know. But I always come back relaxed and thinking clearly. That's a man trip. You get away by yourself, or with some guys. This time you could come with me."

"Me?"

"Why not?" Ledward bumped me with his elbow. "How's about it?"

"A *real* trip?"

"Uh-huh. We could go deep-sea fishing. Fly to the Big Island for the day. I have a friend with a boat."

"Ho! *Really?*"

"The fish will be a little bigger than those aholehole you caught, but I think you can handle it."

"Yeah! Let's do it!"

I could see myself catching a giant fish, tall

as me. But I'd never been on a boat bigger than my small rowboat. Never been on a plane, either.

"I'll give my friend a call tonight, then. Sound good?"

"Yeah! But . . . well, Mom . . ."

Ledward winked. "I'll take care of that part."

Holy moley, deep-sea fishing! That would be so totally awesome! "Thanks, Ledward!"

"No problem."

We stood and started back up toward the house. Ledward held his hand out for the tennis ball. I gave it to him and he tossed it over Streak's head.

Streak ran after it . . . and brought it back halfway.

Ledward chuckled. "Your dog has a sense of humor, I see."

6

KiSS a Bufo

"**D**eep-sea fishing?" Mom said.

The yellow ginger that Ledward had brought her sat in a blue vase on the counter. Stella and Darci were near it, breathing in the sweet smell.

Ledward spread his hands. "It would be good for the boy. Do you remember you met my friend Bill from the Big Island? Well, he's got a boat, and fishing is his specialty."

Mom studied me.

"Calvin has never been on a boat before, let alone on an airplane to get to that boat."

"All the more reason to go."

I couldn't stand it. "Mom, I *want* to go. I've never—"

She held up her hand. "All right, all right, you can go." She grinned at Ledward. "He could use a little man time. All he ever gets is us girls."

A huge smile spread across Ledward's face. "Don't worry, Angela. I'll take good care of him. I was thinking we could go next Saturday."

This was really going to happen! I was so excited I could kiss a bufo! Maybe I'd even try to cut more grass. Yeah, I'd do that.

Like, right now.

But Stella had to butt in.

"Lucky for you wood floats, Stump."

I hated when she called me Stump. I scowled at her.

"Because when you fall off the boat you won't sink." She laughed. "Get it? Stumps float."

"Hardy-har."

"Not hardy-har, party hard, because that's what I'm going to do the minute you walk out the door."

I looked up at Ledward. "Can we go right now?"

7
word Problems

The next day at school I told Mr. Purdy about the trip.

"Wow," he said. "Even if you don't catch any fish you're never going to forget being out on that boat."

He grinned. "I caught a marlin two years

ago. This was along the Kona coast, right where you're going. Hit the line at twelve-fourteen in the afternoon. Boom! *Hoo-ie,* that fish was strong. Took me over three hours to bring it in. Four hundred thirty-two pounds."

"Wow."

Mr. Purdy put his hand on my shoulder. "You know, I just got an idea. Most of your classmates may never get a chance to go deep-sea fishing, even living here in the islands. So what would you think about sharing your experience with us when you get back? Would you be up for that?"

"Sure, Mr. Purdy."

"You're a lucky boy, Calvin."

I thought so, too.

Later that day, I was sitting at my desk, looking out the window and thinking about the trip. I couldn't stop dreaming about it.

"Hi, Calvin," Shayla said.

"Uhnn," I grunted.

Mr. Purdy was on the other side of the room, passing out a math quiz. I didn't want him catching us talking again.

"Did your sister tell you I called you? She said you were taking a bath."

A *bath*!

"I don't take baths. And that wasn't my sister."

"Anyway, I called about homework. But it's all right. I figured it out."

"Good."

I could feel Shayla looking at me, her gaze like the heat off a lightbulb. I made a blinder with my hand on the right side of my face.

Mr. Purdy handed me the quiz.

"Word problems?"

"They're easy," Mr. Purdy said. "And you're a smart boy."

I puffed up my cheeks.

"Shayla," Mr. Purdy said. "You look especially lovely today."

"Thank you, Mr. Purdy."

Mr. Purdy smiled and looked up at the class. "Okay, boot campers, you have ten minutes."

There were five questions. Five!

Mr. Purdy tapped my desk. "Just use your head."

Five minutes later I was only beginning number three.

Shayla slapped down her pencil. "Done."

Show-off.

She took out a piece of paper and started drawing another frog. If she likes frogs so much, I thought, she should come over and dig the bufos out of my grass.

My pencil still hung over question number three.

Shayla sighed, like, It's so hard being smart and finishing my test before everyone else.

I turned in my seat so my back was to her. Saturday's man trip couldn't come soon enough.

8

The MOON

When Saturday finally arrived, Ledward picked me up in the dark before sunrise. I stumbled into my shorts and T-shirt. Ledward had told me not to bring anything. Bill would take care of it.

"My favorite time of day," Ledward said as

we headed down our deserted street in his jeep. "Got the whole world to yourself."

He was right about that. The only other person we saw was a kid on a bike delivering papers.

Mom, Darci, and Stella were still asleep.

Dang. I hadn't asked anyone to feed Streak. I hope you're a good beggar, girl.

Ledward drove up and over the mountains that split the island in half. On the other side, we headed down a green valley with high thin waterfalls that flowed up instead of down. They were hard to see in the dark, but I knew they were there. They flowed upside down because when the water fell, the wind blew it back up.

I sat hunched forward in the open jeep with my arms crossed in the cool morning air. Heat from the engine warmed my feet. Like Ledward, I was only wearing my rubber slippers, shorts, and a T-shirt.

I could hardly wait to get out on that boat.

"I forgot the guy's name who has the boat," I said. "Is it Bad Bill?"

Ledward laughed. "No, but that would work. Everyone calls him Baja. But I like to add the Bill part. Baja Bill sounds more like a sea captain. Anyway, we went to high school together. He's got a head full of stories, so hang on to your hat. Got a head full of knowledge, too." Ledward chuckled. "He'll tell you it's useless knowledge, but it's not. You'll like him."

Cool name. Baja Bill.

We headed down into Honolulu, and finally, to the airport.

The airplane was like a giant tube. We made our way down the aisle to the back. I scooted in next to a window. Ledward sat next to me.

"Does this plane go fast?" I asked.

"Sure does, but when we're up in the air it won't feel like it. It'll be a nice, smooth ride."

We took off as the sun began to lighten the sky. The plane shot up and turned toward the ocean, pressing me into my seat. I squeezed my eyes shut. But when Ledward elbowed me, I slowly peeked out the window.

Ho . . .

Below, I could see the gray-blue morning ocean, and reefs, and big patches of underwater sand, and fishing boats heading out of the harbor, and the edge of the island with all the house lights and roads and buildings and ballparks and rivers.

Man oh man.

I *loved* flying on airplanes! "Look," I said. "We're going higher than the clouds!"

"Yup."

I stared out the window at the ocean until we dropped down out of the sky and landed on the moon.

9

The Kona Coast

Well, it sure *looked* like the moon.

What we really landed on was miles and miles of black rock, with hardly any trees or bushes anywhere. "Is all this rock an old lava flow?" I asked.

"Yep. From back in the eighteen hundreds, I think. Everything you see once flowed red hot down the mountainside. Then it cooled and dried. This island still has an active volcano, but that's way down on the south end. This part is inactive. Or so they say."

The airport sat at the edge of the ocean on all that rock.

Everyone climbed down a stairway that some guys rolled up to the plane. "Wow." I stood at the top looking around. The airport was small compared to the one in Honolulu. And nothing was around it but black rock.

Ledward put on his sunglasses. "A different world here, huh?"

"It's so quiet."

"Who needs noise?"

We walked through the gate and headed out to the road. Ledward nodded up the street. "Here he comes."

"Whoa!" I barked as a truck came toward us hauling a huge boat behind it. "That's Baja Bill?"

"In the flesh."

The truck pulled over and stopped. A

smiling guy in a baseball cap jumped out and met Ledward man-style, thumb to thumb with a shoulder bump. "Long time no see," Baja Bill said. "About time you took a break from that crowded rock you live on."

Ledward laughed. "It's not so bad."

Baja Bill turned to me. "And you must be Tarzan . . . er, I mean Calvin." He crushed my hand when we shook. "You bring us some luck today?"

"Uh . . ."

"You bet," Ledward said. "Beginner's luck."

Baja Bill motioned us toward his truck. "Let's get out of here. We don't want anyone overhearing our fishing secrets."

We drove to a small-boat harbor, the glow

of sunrise growing brighter behind the mountain.

The harbor was a waterway blasted out of the lava rock. Fishermen scurried around silently, loading their boats for the day.

We stopped near a concrete ramp that sloped down into clear green water. Ledward and I got out. Baja Bill turned the truck around and backed the boat into the water.

Boy, I thought. Would my friends love this!

Ledward waded in and held on to the boat so it wouldn't drift away.

There was a name on the back. *Kakalina.*

"It means 'Cathy' in Hawaiian," Ledward said. "Bill's wife."

There were lots of boats in the harbor. They all had funny names, like *Kokomo, Reel Life, Tuna Kahuna, Catch Me If You Can, Something Fishy, Witchy Woman,* and *Goodbye, Charlie.*

And the funniest one, *Snatch Me Bald-Headed.*

Ha!

Baja Bill drove the truck and trailer back up the ramp and parked.

Ledward pulled the *Kakalina* over to a concrete pier. The boat lurched when I jumped aboard. I could feel the watery world through my legs. My knees bent with the slight rocking of the boat.

"Hoo," I whispered.

Ledward grinned. "It's only the beginning, boy."

Five minutes later I was sitting next to Baja Bill in the skipper's seat above the deck, cruising out toward the smoothest, bluest, biggest ocean I had ever seen in my whole entire life.

"Welcome to the Kona coast," Baja Bill said.

"Amazing," I whispered. "Amazing."

10

Violent Creatures

The first thing Baja Bill told me was "You don't drive a boat. You sit at the wheel and pilot it, or you skipper it."

The wheel was like a car's steering wheel. On Baja Bill's boat there were two of them. One was down below inside the cabin and the other was up where we were sitting.

"How come two?" I asked.

Baja Bill chuckled. "Like it up here, do you?"

"Yeah. I can see better."

"That's exactly why I had this boat built like this. I can skipper down below in bad weather, or up here when it's nice, which is most of the time. This is called a flying bridge."

"I like it."

"There are a few important things you need to know about a boat. The right side is called the starboard side, and the left side is called the port side."

I nodded. "Starboard, port."

"The front is the bow, and the back is the stern."

"Okay."

"And the upper edge of the side of a boat is the gunnel, and that bolted-down chair on the deck is the fighting chair."

Ho.

"The captain of a boat is the law. Everyone

follows what he says, even Ledward. That's how it works." Baja Bill tapped an instrument near the wheel. "And check out this gadget. See these jagged lines on the screen?"

"Yeah."

"That's the bottom underneath us. This is a depth finder. See how it falls off here? That shows where the shelf is, where the ocean floor drops quickly from shallow to deep. Of course, you know the islands are just the tops of undersea mountains, right? Volcanoes."

"Mr. Purdy showed us that in class."

"Fascinating, isn't it? So look. If we troll along this shelf we're in a good place to catch some fish. Most likely ono."

"What's ono?"

"A fish that looks kind of like a barracuda. Long, not fat like a tuna. Sharp teeth that look like a saw."

Baja Bill pushed a button on the instrument panel and said, "Be right back."

"But who's going to steer?"

"A compass. I just put it on autopilot. It will steer itself."

Wow. A boat that steers itself.

I sat gazing out over the calm sea. It ran flat all the way out to a razor-sharp horizon. Looking south, I could see the long slope of another mountain in the hazy distance. The island was big, all right. No wonder they called Hawaii the Big Island.

The engines hummed and water whooshed out from under the hull.

Behind me on the deck below, Ledward and Baja Bill set up five fishing lines. "Five delicious meals to choose from," Baja Bill said with a wink. The giant fishing rods had giant reels.

Baja Bill studied the lures in the water behind the boat for a long time, pulling more line off one reel, taking line back on another, until he was satisfied.

Ledward settled into the fighting chair. Baja Bill climbed back up the ladder to the flying bridge. "See anything while I was gone?"

"Just lots of ocean."

Baja Bill flicked off the autopilot and took the wheel.

"I wish my friends could see this," I said. "And my teacher."

"Bring them over. I'll take them out."

"Really?"

"It's my life, Calvin. I love fishing."

"The biggest fish I ever caught was like five inches."

"Well, if we catch something today, it will be bigger than that. Especially if we're lucky enough to hook a marlin."

"What's a marlin?"

Baja Bill looked at me. "Boy, where you been? I can see we have some educating to do here."

Down behind us, Ledward swiveled around in the fighting chair and glanced up. He spread his arms wide. "This is the life!"

Baja Bill gave him a thumbs-up and turned back to me. "So, a marlin is a billfish. Big fish. Sometimes ten, twelve feet long, or more. Maybe you've seen one in the newspaper. Sometimes they put fishing photos in the sports section."

"I think so."

Baja Bill glanced around, as if he were about to tell me a secret. "Listen up. This is serious. You have to be very careful with those

56

guys. They can be extremely dangerous. They can even kill you, if you don't watch out."

I looked at him. "A fish could kill you? I mean, if it's not a shark?"

"Marlin are the most violent creatures in the sea, *worse* than sharks. They eat and attack, eat and attack. That's their life."

"Attack what?"

"Whatever, wherever, however. Fish. Floating logs. Sometimes swimmers and even boats."

Boats!

"I've seen one that weighed in at over sixteen hundred pounds. This was in 1984, a while back. The boat that brought it in was the *Black Bart,* skippered by a guy named Bart Miller. That fish was seventeen feet long! So big they had to drag it back to the harbor behind the boat. No way they could get it aboard."

Baja Bill winked. "No one got hurt bringing that one in, but more than a few boats around here have scars where marlin have rammed their bills into them."

Whoa! Then I grinned. "You're just making this up, right?"

"No, no! I've heard of marlin charging up and leaping right into the boat!"

"Uh . . ."

I looked toward the island. It was a long swim back.

Baja Bill leaned close. "One time when I was 'bout your age, I went fishing with my dad. It was right after a hurricane blew through the islands, and there was a lot of debris in the water. The ocean was still choppy. We were way outside the harbor, *way* out, when we saw something coming toward us in the rolling swells."

"Another boat?"

"Couldn't tell what it was, just this huge *thing* barreling toward us. It made white water

as it moved, so we knew it wasn't just something floating, like a log. It was *alive*."

"Ho," I whispered.

"We had to get out of the way, because it
was going to ram us. So my dad gunned the
engines. Soon we could see what it was—
a giant, angry sperm whale, heading like a
submarine to who knows where.
But here's the thing: that's when
I learned how dangerous a
marlin can be."

"But it was a whale."

Baja Bill nodded. "Sure
was, and when it passed us
we discovered why it was so
angry." Baja Bill sat back and
looked at me. His eyes widened.
"Stuck in its side were not one
but *two* marlins. Rammed their
bills right into that whale and
couldn't get out. They were dead,
and that sperm whale was rag-
ing mad."

59

I gaped at him.

"My guess is they went nuts and attacked the whale for being in their territory."

Baja Bill looked gravely out over the ocean. "So you see, Calvin, you can never let your guard down when you're dealing with a marlin."

"If you do, you could die," I said.

"If you do, you could die."

11

ONO

We headed north along the coast, trolling five lines behind the boat. By then it was around ten o'clock. The sun was clear up over the mountains, and it turned the ocean sparkling blue.

Baja Bill had his back to the wheel and was

studying the wake behind the boat. Whatever was out there, I sure couldn't see it.

"What are you looking at?" I asked.

"Just watching the action of my lures. See the ones way back there, how they jump in and out of the water?"

I squinted. "Not really."

"Keep watching. You'll see them."

Ledward poked his head up to the flying bridge. "Is Bill filling your head with tall tales?"

"You should hear this one about a whale that—"

Ledward put up his hands and laughed. "No, no, not that old one he made up about the sperm whale with the marlins stuck in it?"

I looked at Baja Bill. "It's not true?"

"Of course it's true," Baja Bill said. "Don't listen to him. What does he know? He's a farmer, not a fisherman."

Ledward nodded. "True."

"On the sea, things can happen that you don't expect," Baja Bill went on. "Every day you can get something wild and crazy, or you can just get a long lazy boat ride. You never can tell. That's the thrill of it."

He looked up and eased the boat in closer to shore. "Let's take a serious pass along that undersea shelf I was showing you," he said, tapping the depth finder. "Maybe we can snag an ono."

"Do they attack boats, too?"

"Nah. They're small, not like marlins."

I watched the wake, looking for the lures. All I saw was a bunch of bubbles and white water. After a while I went down on deck and sat in the fighting chair.

The sun was warm, the engines hummed, and the ocean was as smooth as glass. I sure wished my friends could have been there. It kind of surprised me that I hadn't really thought much about them. All I'd been thinking about was what was happening that minute. I was—

Zzzzzzzzz! Zzzzzzzzz!

One of the fishing rods bowed out over the

water. Something had hit a lure. The reel screamed.

Zzzzzzzzzzzzzzzz!

Baja Bill brought the engines to an idle and scrambled down from the flying bridge, Ledward right behind him. The boat rocked in its own wake, exhaust gurgling out the pipes.

Baja Bill grabbed the screaming rod and yanked it out of its chrome holder. "Calvin! Get ready! This one is yours!"

I fell into the fighting chair.

Baja Bill worked the wailing rod over to me and stood it in the rod holder between my legs on the chair. "Hold it here, and here," he said, and showed me how to pull and reel in the line.

I gripped the rod with my left hand and grabbed the

reel handle with my right. I tried to pull the rod back. Whoa! Whatever fish we'd hooked was as strong as a goat!

I pulled back and reeled line in when I bent forward.

Back and forth, inch by inch, bend and reel. I gritted my teeth and puffed out my cheeks.

Ledward put his hand on my shoulder. "Just keep doing what you're doing."

It took ten minutes to get the fish up to the boat. I could see it flashing silver and blue under the surface. It was long, the biggest fish I'd ever seen!

When the leader rose up out of the water, Baja Bill grabbed it with a gloved hand. The leader was made of wire and was attached to the lure. "This leader is wire because fish have sharp teeth!" he said.

Ledward slapped me on the back. "You just caught yourself an ono, Calvin."

I stayed in the chair, stretching to see what the fish looked like.

Baja Bill peered over the gunnel holding

the gaff, a huge steel hook on a pole. He reached over the side and hooked the splashing fish. It thumped the side of the boat. Baja Bill knocked it out with a wooden mallet, then dragged it aboard.

It was wet and shiny and long and silvery with blue stripes. It had about a hundred small, sharp-looking teeth. Good thing the leader was wire.

Baja Bill stuck his hand in its gills and held it up. It was almost as tall as me! *"This,"* he said, "is a nice catch. My guess is it's around forty pounds, and for an ono, that's a big fish."

Ledward opened the fish box built into the deck, and Baja Bill lowered the ono into it. Ledward tore open a bag of ice and spread the ice over the fish.

I couldn't believe I'd just caught it. "He was strong," I said, holding the rod with trembling hands.

Baja Bill grinned. "But you were stronger."

12

Marlin

Baja Bill fired up and headed the *Kakalina* out to deeper sea.

The engines hummed endlessly. It took ten minutes for my hands to stop shaking.

Sometime around noon, I was lounging in the fighting chair watching two dark seabirds skimming the water, looking for food. They flew so smooth and perfect they almost put me to sleep.

Baja Bill got on his radio and called the skipper of another boat. I could hear him talking about where the fish action was that day.

Ledward came up to stand beside me. "Can you believe how close those birds can get to the water?"

"I wish I could fly like that. What are they called?"

"Wedge-tailed shearwater. *'U'au kani* is the Hawaiian name."

"Hey," Baja Bill called from the flying bridge. He pointed. "Look."

About a half mile away, a swirling mass of birds circled the sea. Hundreds. Maybe thousands.

Ledward gave Baja Bill a thumbs-up and hung on to the fighting chair as Bill swung the boat around to head toward the swirling black specks. "Birds like that mean fish."

Within minutes, we were cruising through them. It was the most amazing thing I'd ever seen. Birds everywhere, like a cloud of them. And we were right in the middle of it.

"Talk about a feeding frenzy," Ledward said. "These birds are called noio. They don't skim like your shearwater. These ones dive-bomb."

Boy, did they. From high above, they plunged down into the sea, snatching small fish out of the ocean.

A fish the size of a pocketknife landed on the deck. Then another, and another. "Flying fish," Ledward said, tossing them back into the water. "They're being scared up by bigger fish down below."

We trolled back and forth through the birds, the lures jumping and plunging behind the boat.

Birds swirled around the wake, and—

Bang!

Zzzzzzzzzzzzzzzzzzzzz!

Zzzzzzzzzzzzzzzzzzzzzzzzz!

A reel screamed! The rod bent forward, way more than when the ono had hit. It was an outside rod, starboard side, and it looked like it was about to snap in half.

I jumped out of the fighting chair and scrambled into the cabin to get out of the way.

Baja Bill brought the engines down and Ledward leaped for the jumping rod. Behind the boat, a monster fish burst out of the water, twisting and shaking and turning the water white. It was loosely hooked at the jaw. The lure flopped against its head.

The long bill told me it was a marlin.

"Yai!" I yelped.

The marlin fell back into the ocean with a *whoomp* of exploding water and vanished. Ledward struggled to pull the rod out of its holder. The engines grumbled as the boat rocked.

Baja Bill slid down the ladder from the flying bridge.

Ledward flipped off the clicker on the screaming reel. The reel went silent as line spun out into the water. It was so exciting it was spooky.

The marlin leaped again!

It twisted and shook its head, trying to shake the hook loose. It fell back into the ocean, turned, and rushed toward the boat, thrashing through the water, half in, half out.

"He's coming at us!" Ledward shouted.

Ledward started reeling in the slack line as fast as he could as the marlin charged.

Baja Bill flew up the ladder to the flying bridge and lunged toward the controls.

I froze. Stopped breathing.

The marlin went under, then leaped again, completely out of the water and so close I could look it in the eye.

The engines roared to life. The boat jumped

ahead as the bow rose up out of the water.

The marlin charged under the boat, taking the line with it.

Ledward hung on to the reel with one hand and the fighting chair with the other.

The boat swerved as Bill tried to get out in front of the fish again.

Just then Ledward fell back.

The line went limp.

"Dang!" Baja Bill yelled from the bridge. "Dang, dang, dang!"

That big fish was gone.

"What happened?" I asked, gulping air.

Ledward wiped sweat from his neck. "Prop cut the line."

Baja Bill brought the boat down to a crawl. No one spoke.

I gaped at the ocean where the giant fish had been, the surface now a small smooth whirlpool. Looking over the gunnel into the depths, I saw spears of sunlight shooting down toward the bottom of the deep, deep sea. The color was a blue I'd never seen before.

It scared me.

The boat rocked, idling.

The swirling mass of birds moved on, now a quarter mile away.

"Too bad," Ledward said. "He was a nice one. What you think he weighed, Bill?"

"Two-fifty. About."

Ledward nodded and looked at me. "How you doing?"

"Uh . . . okay . . . I think."

Baja Bill grunted. "Hang on to your hat, kid, because I'm not done here. No, sir, I am surely not done with this."

13

The Black Mariah

Baja Bill went to work.

He was so excited that now even *his* hands were shaking. He squatted down and dug through a box in the hold. He found what he was looking for and sat back on his heels.

He held it up. "This will get her."

It was another lure. This one was black as

night. Points of light, like stars, sparkled in its huge head. It had rubber hanging on it like a hula skirt, with a giant steel hook poking through.

I stepped closer, gaping at the monster lure. It was creepy.

"Secret weapon," he said. "My trusty old Black Mariah."

Baja Bill grinned. "Here, see this? Only one hook. If you use two, they could pin its jaws shut. If the fish gets off the line, you don't want to take the chance of killing it."

The steel hook looked strong enough to pull Ledward's jeep.

Ledward put his hand on my shoulder. "This is where Baja Bill turns into Captain Ahab."

"Who's Captain Ahab?"

"Guy on a mission. He's from a great book called *Moby-Dick*."

"Cool." For sure I was going to read it. Maybe Mr. Tanaka had it in the school library.

Baja Bill tied a new double line to a new swivel and secured it to the big black lure.

"The swivel keeps the line from getting all wound up," he said. "That old fish can jump and turn all he wants, no problem."

This time the leader wasn't wire but extra-thick fishing line.

"Kick her into gear, would ya, Led?"

Ledward went up to the bridge and moved the throttle forward.

As the boat came up to speed, Baja Bill dropped the Mariah overboard and released the drag on the reel. When the lure was far behind the boat, he stopped the running line and tugged a few inches more off the reel until the lure was exactly where he wanted it.

"The way that fish was jumping around, my guess is he was showing off for some female, and with marlin, it's the female that gets big, not the male. We're going after his girl-friend, boy."

"That one wasn't big?"

"There's bigger ones."

I glanced up at Ledward. He gave me a grin and a thumbs-up.

"Can you see the lure I just put out?" Baja Bill asked.

"I think so. By the third wave in the wake?"

Baja Bill clapped my back. "Good eyes. You're catching on."

The new lure plunged, smoked, and wiggled. If any lure was going to grab a marlin's attention, it would be that one.

"We're coming to find you, Big Mama," Baja Bill said to the sea.

The engines thrummed as we circled back toward the birds. Ocean water hissed out from under the hull.

Baja Bill looked up at Ledward. "Let's trade places. If we get another hit, we need you down here. I'm feeling lucky. I'm thinking big."

Ledward set the wheel on autopilot and climbed down as Baja Bill went up.

Ledward stood watching the lures with his

knees braced up against the stern gunnel. I sat in the chair, ready to jump out if anything happened.

Deep-sea fishing was something else! It grabbed you and took you away. When it was boring and nothing was happening, you sat there thinking about what *could* happen. And then when something did happen, your mind was on the fish and nothing else in the whole entire universe. Nothing.

I was hooked. Just like a fish.

I couldn't wait to tell my friends about it. Mom and Darci, too.

I watched the Black Mariah work behind the boat. Baja Bill set four other lines out, too, all of them plunging and leaving smoky trails of bubbles in the wake.

We ran through the birds again. Flying fish thumped onto the deck.

I thought I saw something in the water and stretched to look harder. There was a huge dark shadow in the wake. "Ledward!"

I said, stumbling out of the fighting chair. "Look!"

Just as he turned, the ocean erupted!

A bill and a huge head came out of the water—and a fierce eye.

The marlin rose . . . and rose and rose. The neon-blue bars on its side glistened, and when it fell back into the sea, the ocean around it thundered, turned white, and *whoomp*ed out in every direction.

"Jeese!" I gasped.

Seconds later, a reel screamed.

This marlin was bigger by far than the one we'd lost, and it was tearing away toward the horizon, taking Baja Bill's Black Mariah with it!

Big Mama

Ledward fought the rod out of its chrome holder. The marlin was too big, too fast. He could barely stagger the rod over to the fighting chair.

I tried to get out of his way, fell, and hit my elbow on the bench seat.

Baja Bill slammed the throttle down,

slowing the boat. The stern rose in the oncoming wake. The reel kept screaming as the marlin ran away with more and more line. Sweat rolled down Ledward's grimacing red face.

Baja Bill jumped off the ladder onto the deck. He grabbed my arm and helped me up. "You okay?"

I nodded.

He pointed off the back of the boat. "Watch. Keep your eyes right there. She's going to come up."

"How do you know?"

"I know."

Ledward bent forward, gripping the rod, now alive with line still racing off the reel. More and more and more.

Far behind the boat the marlin leaped fully out of the water, its tail slashing the air. It was so big I could hardly believe my eyes.

"Big *Mama*!" Baja Bill shouted.

The wild run soon slowed, and Ledward managed to fall back into the chair and start the fight.

Baja Bill wrapped a harness around Ledward's lower back and clipped it to hooks on the reel. "You're going to need this with that one. She could break your back, you don't watch out."

Ledward grimaced. "In fifteen places."

The harness was only clipped to the reel. If the fish was strong enough, could it pull Ledward into the ocean?

He hauled back on the rod, teeth clenched. Veins bulged in his neck. He reeled line in when he fell forward. Gaining an inch here, an inch there. Bit by bit. Pull and reel. Over and over, until he was so sweaty it looked as if he'd just climbed out of the ocean.

Baja Bill scooped a bucket of water out of the sea and sponged Ledward's head to cool him off.

Ledward kept fighting.

Baja Bill grinned at me. "He's going to feel like he's been hit by a truck tomorrow morning."

Ledward grunted.

For the next two hours, Ledward fought that fish closer and closer. Baja Bill went back and forth to the wheel, keeping the line directly off the back of the boat, never letting it run to one side or the other.

I climbed up to the bridge and stood near him, looking down on Ledward and the sea behind us. I could see the marlin underwater, keeping pace, a huge dark monster on the port side.

"Leader's coming up!" Ledward shouted. "Get down here!"

Baja Bill put the boat on slow autopilot and I followed him down to the deck. With both hands on my shoulders, he bent over and looked me in the eye. "We're going to need your help, Calvin. This is a three-man job, minimum. I'm going to ask you to do something you've never done in your life. You haven't even dreamed of it. I'm going to ask you to tag a nine-hundred-pound fish. By yourself."

Stick and Knife

Baja Bill handed me a razor-sharp boat knife. I turned it toward the sun. It had nicks in the blade. It had been used a lot. I hadn't done one thing, and already my hands were shaking.

"And this," he said, holding up a pole with a small flaglike thing on its tip, "is your tag stick. I'll tell you what to do with it when the time comes. Tell you what to do with the knife, too. You ready?"

I nodded, not ready at all. What was tagging? What was the knife for?

Baja Bill took off his watch and stuck it in his pocket. A band of white skin circled his tanned wrist. He dug around in a drawer and pulled out a pair of tough canvas gloves with long cuffs that went halfway up to his elbows.

He looked over at Ledward. "How's she feel?"

"Hopefully, we have an understanding."

Baja Bill pulled me close and pointed toward the marlin gliding just behind the boat in the clear water. Sunlight flashed on her flank. "See those stripes? That she still has them means she's far from finished, and that's just where we want her."

The marlin looked longer than Mom's car. Its tail alone wouldn't fit in the fish hold, where we'd put the ono. "How you going to get it on the boat? It's so big."

"We're not. We're going to tag her and turn her loose. That's where you come in."

Man oh man oh man oh man.

"Okay, Led," Baja Bill said. "Bring that leader up to where I can reach it, slowly now."

Ledward pulled back on the rod, using his back and the harness, then turned the reel lightly. Nobody wanted to see that giant fish go crazy again.

Baja Bill braced his knees up against the gunnel and leaned over the water. He took the leader in one hand and pulled smoothly toward his chest.

The marlin moved closer to the boat.

Baja Bill reached out with his other hand, wrapped the leader around his fist, and slowly drew the marlin closer. "Okay, Calvin. Bring the knife and the stick and come stand next to me."

I braced my knees against the gunnel like he did.

"Now, listen," Baja Bill said. "We've got to do this right."

I gripped the knife in one hand and the tag stick in the other. "Ready."

"Good. Stand by till I tell you to move."

Baja Bill pulled the fish closer, and closer. "Led, back off on the drag a little. Give me a foot or two of line. Okay now, Calvin. I'm going to walk this fish forward, and I want you to set the tag. What you're going to do is firmly poke the point of that stick into the side of the fish, just at the shoulder, by her dorsal fin. Poke it in and pull the stick back. The tag will stay in the fish—and don't worry. She won't feel it. Don't move till I tell you, okay?"

"Okay."

Nothing else in the world existed but that fish. Blood pounded in my temples.

"Steady," Baja Bill said quietly.

He pulled the marlin closer. Its bill, huge head, and back broke the surface, rising up just below me. I could have reached out and touched it.

"Now!" Baja Bill commanded.

I jabbed the stick into the fish and pulled it

back. The tag, like a small flag, lay wet against the flesh. I dropped the stick to the deck.

"Now," Baja Bill said. "Grab the lure, slide it up the leader, then take that knife and cut the leader as close to the hook as you can."

"Me?"

I stared at the eye of the fish, holding my breath.

"You can do it, just reach out and grab the lure. I've got her under control. Don't think about it. Just do it."

I looked at the marlin.

"You want to touch her first?"

"The fish?"

"Go ahead."

I reached over and placed my hand on her side. "Ho," I whispered. "She's warm."

"Blood gets hot in all that fighting." Baja Bill smiled. "All right, cut her loose."

I pulled the lure up and held it, then slipped the blade under the thick leader and cut the line. The hook stayed in the marlin's bony jaw as the fish drifted away from the boat. The hook looked small, like an earring. The marlin probably didn't even know it was there.

Ledward climbed out of the fighting chair and stood next to us holding the rod.

The three of us watched as the monster fish sank. It woke, realizing it was free, and surged down, diving into the deep blue sea.

Down, down, down.

Gone.

"That hook will fall out within a week," Baja Bill said.

Ledward grunted. "And I'll be asleep in five minutes."

I looked at the knife in my hand. I did it. I actually *did* it.

Ledward and Baja Bill both grinned at me. "You one of us now," Ledward said. "A fisherman. A real one."

16

Sharks

"Hey," Ledward said, waking me an hour later. "You enjoying yourself out here on the ocean?"

I'd just scarfed lunch down like a starving dog, then dozed in the chair. "Yeah, I love it. In fact, I've got an idea. How about we stay here a week?"

"I wish . . . but we have that six o'clock flight."

I looked out over the sea. "I could do this all day and all night, and then do it again the next day, and the next one after that."

Baja Bill called down from the bridge. "Any time you want, you just give me a call. All I need is a day to prepare."

"We'll do this again," Ledward said. "But your mama needs to get used to having you gone first. I bet she hasn't stopped worrying since we left."

"Why?"

"How moms are."

It seemed like we'd left home days ago.

Baja Bill put the boat on autopilot and climbed down. He dug bottles of water out of the cooler and handed them around. "This was not what I'd call a normal day out fishing, Calvin. Usually it's a long quiet boat ride. But today, you brought us luck."

"And," Ledward added, tapping my chest with a finger, "you caught our dinner."

I'd almost forgotten about the ono.

Baja Bill took out his watch, glanced at it, and put it back on. "Better head back. You got a plane to catch."

We reeled in all the lures and coiled them up with their leaders. When we were finished, Ledward leaned back on a seat and closed his eyes. "Wake me if I fall asleep."

"What you mean, if?" Baja Bill said.

Ledward grunted.

Baja Bill nudged me. "Come sit with me."

I followed him up the ladder.

He kicked the boat off autopilot and brought the engines up. We swung around and sped toward the harbor. It felt great to go fast after a day of slow trolling.

"You did a fine job, Calvin. You can be my deckhand anytime."

"Really?"

"You bet."

We rode in silence a few minutes before he spoke again.

"Once I was out with a guy from Montana.

Nice guy. We were about a quarter mile south of here and a lot farther out, and we hooked an ahi, and not a small one, either."

"That's a tuna, right?"

"Right, but not just any tuna. This one was a *big* tuna. It was late in the day. We were headed back to the harbor, like now, and *boom!* That fish hit like a hammer. But we didn't see it like we saw the marlin today. No, this one sounded, went straight down. My angler grabbed the reel and tried his best to stop it from going deeper, but that fish just kept on going, because it took a small lure on a light line."

"Wow."

Baja Bill waved at another boat that was also heading toward the harbor. The skipper waved back.

"How deep did it go?"

"Deep. When it finally stopped going down, the pressure on the line alone made it feel like we'd hooked a garbage truck. That light line was as tight as steel. I told the guy, forget it, you'll never get that fish back up. Cut the line and let's go home. But the guy said he didn't come here to hook a fish and then cut the line."

Baja Bill chuckled.

"Well, if you didn't see the fish, how'd you know it was a tuna?"

"Just a guess . . . until we saw it."

"He got it back up?"

Baja Bill nodded. "Sure did. And you know what came up with it? Sharks. White-tips, scariest creatures in the ocean. We figured that tuna died from the pressure of going so deep, and as my angler worked it back up, those sharks discovered an easy dinner. All we pulled aboard was the head."

Ho! What a story!

"It took the guy a couple-three hours to get that fish head up to the boat. We pulled into the harbor after dark. Believe it or not, my angler took that ahi's head home and had it mounted!"

Baja Bill humphed, as if that were the craziest thing ever.

"Today it sits over his fireplace somewhere in Montana. He sent me a picture of it, and on the back he wrote: *Next time we're going to catch the rest of this fish!*"

I laughed.

Baja Bill reached over and messed up my hair with his hand. "Find your dream and live it, Calvin. What's your life worth if you don't do that?"

Deep-sea fishing might be my dream, I thought.

"I have a question," I said. "Why did we let that marlin go?"

"I was wondering when you'd get around to that. You see, most anglers who come to fish off the Kona coast would want to keep a big fish like that, if only to get their picture taken standing next to it. But to me, that's not a good enough reason to kill a big fish. They're beautiful creatures. To fight it and win? That's enough. Unless you fish as a business and sell it for food, there's no need to kill something with so much life in it. Agree?"

I thought for a moment. "Yeah. It was too big, anyway."

"Ha!"

"Okay, but why did we stick a tag on it?"

"Research. Each tag is bar-coded. When we get back to the harbor, I'll fill out a form with the same code. I'll record the date, the location, and the size of the fish and send it in. When someone catches a fish with a tag he reports it, then you get the information on the tag and you know how much it's grown and where it's gone."

Research? Mr. Purdy would be interested in that.

"A while back, a guy here hooked a small marlin and tagged it. He guessed it was about a hundred pounds. He turned it loose, and a year later someone caught that same fish way down in the South China Sea. It weighed around two hundred fifty pounds. So people who study fish got some good information."

"Wow."

"All life is amazing, Calvin."

I nodded. I'd never thought about that before.

"You ready to go home and face that bufo problem Ledward said you had? Mow that lawn?"

"He told you about that?"

"Some girl problem, too?"

"*What?*"

"Don't worry. Your secrets are safe with me."

17

The Frog

The bufos down by the river were croaking loudly when Ledward and I got home that night. I was so tired I could hardly get out of the jeep.

Streak leaped around us like a flea. I scooped her up with a grunt. The driveway rocked gently, my mind still thinking I was on the boat. "Looks like you missed me, huh, girl?"

She licked my face.

One thing about dogs: they're always really happy to see you.

As the light in the garage popped on, Ledward grabbed the ice chest we'd borrowed from Baja Bill. The cleaned ono sat wrapped in butcher paper on a bed of dry ice.

Mom and Darci came out, Darci with a chocolate ice cream cone. I was so hungry I could have eaten the box the cones came in.

"I was beginning to worry about you two," Mom said, giving me a hug. "So how did your man day go?"

"It was awesome,

Mom. I caught an ono! That's a big fish that looks like a barracuda, and you can also call it a wahoo. We got it in here." I tapped the ice chest.

Mom peeked inside. "Whoa," she said. "That's a lot of fish!"

"This boy was born for fishing," Ledward said. "He's a real angler."

Darci pulled on my T-shirt. "Did you like going on a plane, Calvin?"

"Yeah. It was cool."

Like I flew on planes all the time. No big deal.

Darci grinned. "Me and Mom are going to fly to Kauai."

"You'll like it, Darce."

Mom smiled and pulled Darci close. "You men must be hungry."

"I could eat this entire fish," Ledward said. "But it's late. How's about tomorrow I come over, put it on the grill with lemon and butter?"

"It's a date," Mom said.

While Ledward packed the fish into the

freezer and some in the fridge for the next day, Mom made us toast and fried eggs on rice. I gobbled mine down with shoyu—what Willy calls soy sauce. Nothing could have tasted better.

As I ate, I looked around.

"Where's Stella?"

"At the movies with Clarence."

Dang. I wanted her to see I caught a fish. I wanted Clarence to see it, too.

After we ate, Mom brought out some cookies. "So, did you get pictures of your trip?"

Pictures?

She looked at Ledward. "You *did* bring a camera, didn't you?"

"Oops," he said.

Mom stared at him.

Then at me.

Then back at Ledward. "The biggest thing Calvin has done since he went to see Johnny at the auditorium and you didn't take a camera?"

Johnny was my dad—Little Johnny Coconut, a famous singer who had a hit song called

"I Love Sunshine Pop." He and my mom were divorced, and now he lived in Las Vegas.

Ledward opened his hands. "Forgot."

"No," Mom said. "You didn't forget, because it was never in your head to begin with."

Ledward gave me a guilty look. "Sorry," he said. "I should–"

"I've got it all right here, Mom," I said, tapping my head.

Mom sighed.

"Got to say good night," Ledward said, pulling his keys out of his pocket. "I'm beat."

As we walked Ledward out through the garage, I saw a note stuck under my garage-bedroom door.

I grabbed it.

"What's that?" Mom asked.

I unfolded it. And groaned.

Hi, Calvin.

> *Here's a frog for you. Without a bow.*
> *Do you like it?*
>
> > *Your friend, you know who*

I handed Mom the paper.

"How cute. Who's your friend?"

"Uh . . . a girl."

"Shayla?"

I frowned. "She won't leave me alone, Mom."

"She must like you, and I don't blame her. You're a sweetheart."

"Mom!"

Ledward took the drawing from Mom. He looked up and winked at me.

Great.

18

Partner up

"Did you get my note, Calvin?"

It was Monday morning. I'd spent Sunday trying to tell Julio and Willy about my man trip. They shrugged it off, like, okay . . . so?

They'd missed out on something big, so I guess I could understand why they didn't get too excited about it. And maybe I sounded like I was bragging. But I'd tried not to.

Anyway, I was sitting at my desk with Shayla glancing over to catch my eye so she could say something. I didn't want my friends to see and make fun of it later.

Shayla reached over and poked my arm. "Well?"

"Why'd you come to my house?" I said it low, so Mr. Purdy wouldn't hear.

"I didn't. I gave the note to Maya to give to you."

"Okay, fine, but . . . *why?*" I whispered a little too loud.

Ace, who sat behind us, inched closer.

I scooted my desk forward.

Shayla didn't seem to care about Ace. "So, did you?"

"Did I *what?*"

"Get my note."

Go away!

Shayla wouldn't stop. "I still want to know

about the place you got your dog. Can you show me how to get there?"

I wanted to yell, Please, Mr. Purdy, start the class! Give us math, give us geography, give us word problems, just do it *now!*

"Ask your mom to take you," I mumbled.

"She can't. She works."

"Your dad, then."

Shayla just looked at me, and I remembered Maya once said Shayla didn't have a dad.

I frowned at my desk.

Shayla sat saying nothing for once.

I thought: Man trip, man trip. Think of fishing. The big marlin came to mind. And the whale with the bills in it. And me in the fighting chair. Ho, yeah! What an awesome day!

"Why are you smiling, Calvin?" Shayla asked.

"Mr. Purdy," I said, raising my hand. "Aren't we supposed to start class now?"

Mr. Purdy looked up from the papers he

was sorting. He glanced at the clock. "You're right, Calvin. I didn't know you liked boot camp so much."

"Oh yeah, Mr. Purdy, I want to study stuff."

Mr. Purdy grinned. "I like that enthusiasm. Keep it up."

Boot camp was what he called our fourth-grade class, because Mr. Purdy had been in the army. Every third grader in school prayed they would get into Mr. Purdy's boot camp.

"All right, class, listen up. We have a special assignment today, one that involves team-work."

The second he said *teamwork* I glanced over at Willy, Maya, Rubin, and Julio. My team.

"But first," Mr. Purdy went on, "Calvin is going to tell us about his trip to the Big Island."

"Uh . . . what?"

"Remember we talked about that?"

"Oh. Right."

Mr. Purdy sat on his desk and crossed his arms. "Stand up and face the class, Calvin. So we can hear you better. And speak up. We don't want Rubin falling asleep back there."

Rubin pumped his fist in the air.

I stood. "Yeah, um. On Saturday I went on a plane to the Big Island."

When I said *plane* the class mumbled things like Awesome; Ho, I like go on one, too.

I decided to make my story more exciting.

"The plane was fast! Like a rocket! And then we were so high I could see the whole is-land at one time, and I could look down into the ocean and see boats and reefs and stuff swimming around, like sharks and stingrays. And then, when we got to the Big Island . . . we landed on a lava flow."

That caused some grins.

I nodded, getting into it. "And then I went fishing on a boat almost as long as this *room*."

Everyone looked around, nodding.

"And I caught a fish called an ono, which looks like a barracuda, and if you know about fish it's also called a wahoo."

"Wa-hooo!" Rubin called.

Everyone laughed, even Mr. Purdy.

"And we caught a marlin, a gigantic one— that's a big fish with a bill like a spear on its nose. Man, that thing jumped all the way out of the water, and it was as big as a truck! It was so *awesome*! But those fish are dangerous, you know. They stab whales and get their bills stuck in them and die, and if they feel like it they can jump into your boat and kill you, too."

Some kids whooped and slapped high fives.

"Calvin," Mr. Purdy said. "Let's try to keep the fish tales within the range of believability."

"Huh?"

"So how big was the marlin?" Mr. Purdy asked. "How much did it weigh?"

I scrunched my face. "Well, Baja Bill said it was about eight hundred pounds."

"Wow!" the whole class said.

"But we let it go. After I tagged it. You know, for research."

"You tagged it yourself?" Mr. Purdy asked.

"Uh-huh, and I cut the line and saved the lure, too. With a knife."

Mr. Purdy nodded. "Good! That's what I'd do, Calvin. I'd let it go."

"Yeah, why kill it? Unless you make a living as a fisherman. And guess what? I touched it!" For a second, I remembered the marlin's heat, its power. "It was . . ."

How could I even describe it?

Mr. Purdy slid off his desk. "It was an amazing day! Thank you, Calvin. That was very interesting. Now," he said with a clap of his hands. "The special project: Mr. Purdy's Awareness Walk."

I sat down.

In my head I was still on the *Kakalina*.
There was a lot more I wanted to say, like
about the tuna head, and the sharks, and the
marlin that got away.

Shayla smiled at me.

"There were birds, too," I mumbled as I sat
back down.

Mr. Purdy went on. "With a partner, you
will take a notebook outside and walk around
the schoolyard and record all that you see. You
can write down things you think about, too.
The idea is to be more aware of what sur-
rounds you, and how you respond to it. Often
we just go through our lives without even no-
ticing the world around us. I want you to stop
and smell the roses."

Roses? All we had outside was weeds.

"We'll work in teams of two," Mr. Purdy
said.

The class erupted. Everyone turned to call
or wave to a friend. I tried to catch somebody's
eye.

"Sssss," Mr. Purdy hissed, for silence. "Settle

down, boot campers. I've already worked it out. Partner up with the person next to you."

Next to—

No, Mr. Purdy, no.

"One of you will make the observations and the other will record them. Talk with your partner and decide who will do what. We'll head outside in two minutes."

Shayla grabbed her notebook and pencil. "I'll record and you observe." She smiled and stood up. "Well?"

19

Brown Rubber Slipper

What a weird project.

Who creeps around their school looking at stuff? And while I was staring at weeds, guys like Baja Bill were out fishing. Who's got the better deal?

"Uhh . . . no-brainer," I mumbled.

Shayla looked at me. "What?"

"Huh?"

She shrugged, and stuck to me like a shadow. "What should I write down, Calvin? There's so much."

"So much?" I glanced around. "There's nothing."

"Sure there is," she said. "We can write down: *buildings, trees, grass, dirt, sky, walkways, the cafeteria.* Lots of stuff."

"How boring is that? It's stuff that's always here. There's nothing new."

"Mr. Purdy didn't say to just write new things."

"He said to smell the roses. And I don't see any."

"Let's go out by the back fence," Shayla said. "Maybe we can find something new there."

I squinted at her.

Shayla smiled.

On the other side of the big fence was a big field. Beyond that was the middle school. "You could write down: *old fence, big field,* and *middle school,* I guess."

"*Those* are new?" Shayla said.

I eyed her. "*You* find something new, then."

She tapped her pencil on her teeth. "Um . . . how about *different,* instead of new?"

"Like what?"

She shrugged. "You find it. You're really smart."

I crossed my arms and gave her big-time stink eye. "Are you making fun of me?"

Her jaw dropped. "I'd never do that!"

I studied her.

"I *do* think you're smart."

She was telling the truth. I could tell. Shayla wasn't mean. She showed off. She sat up too straight. She always raised her hand right away. She drew dumb frogs on everything.

But Shayla was never mean.

I looked away. "Okay. Write down . . . um." I looked down. "Ants."

Shayla squatted down to look. "Good!" She wrote *ants* in her notebook. "What else?"

I got down next to her and looked closer. "Cock-a-roach. There. See it? And a nickel." I stuck it in my pocket.

 Shayla wrote them down.

"Rust on the fence? Mynah birds, doves. Sleeping grass. A soda can. And this." I pinched up a cigarette butt.

"Yick."

I dropped it.

Shayla scribbled that down and waited for more. That was when I noticed: Shayla wasn't being pushy. She wasn't bothering me.

"What else, Calvin?"

I looked around. Out in the field I spotted a rubber slipper. Weird. How could you lose one slipper and keep on going?

"One brown rubber slipper."

"Oh, that's good how you added *brown*." She wrote it down.

"How about *lost* brown rubber slipper?"

"Yeah, lost!"

I smiled. Then caught myself and scowled.

"So you went fishing," Shayla said. "Was it fun? What you said in class was really interesting."

I looked at her. "You like deep-sea fishing?"

"Maybe. I've never been on a fishing boat. But if I caught a fish, I could never kill it. I'd let it go. Just like you did."

I puffed up. "Yeah. To fight and catch a fish is enough. Then you throw it back. How could you take a fish as beautiful as a marlin from the sea?"

I winced. Did I really say *beautiful*? Guys don't say something is beautiful. Had Baja Bill said that?

Shayla stopped and turned to me. "What did you just say?"

"Uh . . . to fight a fish is enough?"

"No, you said it was beautiful."

"Hey!" I shouted, spotting Julio and Maya. I turned and headed toward them.

Shayla hurried to catch up. "That was a really nice thing to say, Calvin. About the fish."

"Don't tell anyone I said that, okay?"

"Why?"

"It's embarrassing, that's why, so just don't."

"Okay, it's our secret."

I stopped. "Really? You won't tell?"

"Never." She pulled a zipper across her lips with her fingers.

20

Seventeen Bufos

At home that afternoon after school, I stood in the yard with Streak. The lawn mower was exactly where I'd left it days ago. If I waited even one more hour the grass would be impossible to cut, maybe even with a tractor. We'd have to fence it off and bring in the cows.

Also, I felt bad that Mom had to keep

telling me to do it. Ledward was right. She did count on me to help around the house.

"I've run out of time, Streak. I gotta do it. Want to help me look for bufos?"

Streak tilted her head.

I puffed up my cheeks and blew the air out slowly.

Streak sniffed the grass and jumped when a toad leaped out and headed toward the river. Streak barked and followed it. The toad disappeared into the swamp grass.

I toed out three of them and watched Streak bark them to the river.

It took ten minutes just to get the lawn mower started. It coughed to life, the noise roaring through our peaceful neighborhood like a jet flying super-low. Streak ducked her head and shrank around to the back of the house.

Pushing the

mower into that thick grass was like riding a ten-speed bike on the beach.

The biggest toad I'd seen in my life leaped out of the grass in front of me and charged downhill. Scared me spitless!

There were *still* bufos in the grass.

I shut the engine off.

It was so quiet, just like when we got off Baja Bill's boat.

"All right, toads. Wake up. All of you."

I started searching with my feet.

"Ack!"

I squatted down to dig out the squishy thing under my bare foot. It was way down where the grass was wet. I pried it out and picked it up. It was soft and rubbery, with a beating heart. I stared into its face. "Were you ever in an alien movie?"

It blinked.

"I know someone who thinks you guys are cute."

I stood.

"Bye-bye," I said, and reached my arm

back to throw Mr. Bufo into the river.

I stopped and looked at him again.

And you know what? He smiled at me. No joke. The look on his face was like, Howzit? Or Wassup?

Jeese.

"So maybe Tito had it wrong, huh?" I said.

I carried him to the water and let him swim out of my hand.

Seventeen.

That's how many I carried to the river.

Seventeen smiling bufos who didn't get shredded, whose guts did not end up on my feet.

And then I cut the grass.

21

The Brotherhood of Men

That night Ledward came over for another night of ono, cooked on the hibachi. This time he marinated it in shoyu, sugar, and ginger, and boy, was it good.

And of course, me and Ledward told Mom,

Darci, and Stella about our incredible day with Baja Bill all over again.

Stella said we were boring her to death and went to her room.

Darci yawned and turned on the TV.

Only Mom listened to all of it.

At bedtime, I flipped off the light and climbed to the top bunk. Streak curled up on the bunk below. Even she was tired of hearing about our man trip.

I lay on my side in the dark, looking out the window.

The moon cast long night shadows across the driveway and Ledward's jeep. The sweet smell of fresh-cut grass drifted in through the screen.

I had a front-row seat for the sounds of a bazillion insects and other creatures that took over the neighborhood at night, probably even the seventeen toads I'd rescued.

Some guys I knew would laugh their heads off if they ever heard about that. Rescuing *toads*? Next thing you knew I'd be calling them beautiful. Man, was I losing it.

But so what? Toads deserved to live, too.

Shayla would go nuts if she ever heard I'd tossed some in the river.

Someone came out the kitchen door into the garage.

Ledward headed out to his jeep and got in. For a minute, he sat back and looked out toward the yard.

He got out and walked toward my window. Quietly, he said, "Boy. You still awake?"

"Yeah."

"Come outside."

I slipped off my bunk and went outside. "What?"

"You did it," Ledward said. "You cut the grass."

"I had to. I don't know anybody who has cows."

Ledward laughed. "Sorry if I woke you."

"I was just lying there listening to the bugs."

"Quite a symphony, huh?"

I nodded.

"What did you do with the bufos in the grass?"

"Found them with my feet and let them go in the river. I guess throwing them could . . . you know, like you said . . . hurt them."

We stood looking at the moonlit river.

Toads croaked, bugs buzzed. It all felt so much closer in the dark, a whole different world. It was alive. I could almost feel the bellies of the bufos I'd held. Soft, with beating hearts. And warm, like the marlin.

"All that life out there." Ledward put his hand on my shoulder. "Pretty amazing."

I listened.

"Hey," Ledward said. "You want to take a walk?"

"Now? In the dark?"

"Why not?"

I grinned. "Yeah. Why not?"

We headed down the street. Lights were still on down at Julio's house, but most of the houses were dark. It was fun to go for a walk when everyone else was falling asleep.

Ledward walked with his hands in the pockets of his shorts. "You get your girl problems taken care of?"

"Maybe. I guess."

"They get you coming and going, don't they?"

"You can run but you can't hide." Stella said that to me all the time. I wasn't too sure what it meant, but I liked it.

Ledward laughed, loud.

It was me and him, on another man trip. Sometimes you go fishing. Sometimes you just go for a walk.

Toads kept croaking. Bugs kept buzzing.
All that life.
Ledward was right.
It *was* amazing.

A Hawaii Fact:

Of the six hundred active volcanoes on earth today, Kilauea Volcano, on the Big Island of Hawaii, is the world's largest and most active.

A Calvin Fact:

Your nose and ears continue growing throughout your entire life. Think about it: what if you lived to be 150?

Graham Salisbury is the author of six other Calvin Coconut books: *Trouble Magnet*, *The Zippy Fix*, *Dog Heaven*, *Zoo Breath*, *Hero of Hawaii*, and *Kung Fooey*, as well as several novels for older readers, including the award-winning *Lord of the Deep*, *Blue Skin of the Sea*, *Under the Blood-Red Sun*, *Eyes of the Emperor*, *House of the Red Fish*, and *Night of the Howling Dogs*. Graham Salisbury grew up in Hawaii. Calvin Coconut and his friends attend the same school Graham did—Kailua Elementary School. Graham now lives in Portland, Oregon, with his family. You can visit him on the Web at grahamsalisbury.com.

Jacqueline Rogers has illustrated more than ninety books for young readers over the past twenty years. She studied illustration at the Rhode Island School of Design. You can visit her on the Web at jacquelinerogers.com.